Spike & Cubby's ICE CREAM ISLAND ADVENTURE

by Heather Sellers

illustrated by Amy L. Young

Henry Holt and Company
New York

214 4422

Henry Holt and Company, LLC
Publishers since 1866
115 West 18th Street
New York, New York 10011
www.henryholt.com

Henry Holt is a registered trademark of Henry Holt and Company, LLC
Text copyright © 2004 by Heather Sellers
Illustrations copyright © 2004 by Amy L. Young
All rights reserved. Distributed in Canada by H. B. Fenn and Company Ltd.

Library of Congress Cataloging-in-Publication Data
Sellers, Heather
Spike and Cubby's Ice Cream Island adventure / Heather Sellers; illustrated by Amy L. Young.
Summary: Two dogs, Spike and Cubby, get caught in a storm while trying to sail to their dream destination—
the grand opening of Ice Cream Island.
[1. Dogs—Fiction. 2. Storms—Fiction. 3. Sailing—Fiction.] I. Young, Amy, ill. II. Title.
PZ7.S45698Sp 2004   [E]—dc22   2003022499

ISBN 0-8050-6910-0 / EAN 978-0-8050-6910-5
First Edition—2004 / Designed by Patrick Collins
The artist used gouache on Fabriano Uno soft-press watercolor paper to create the illustrations for this book.
Printed in the United States of America on acid-free paper. ∞
1 3 5 7 9 10 8 6 4 2

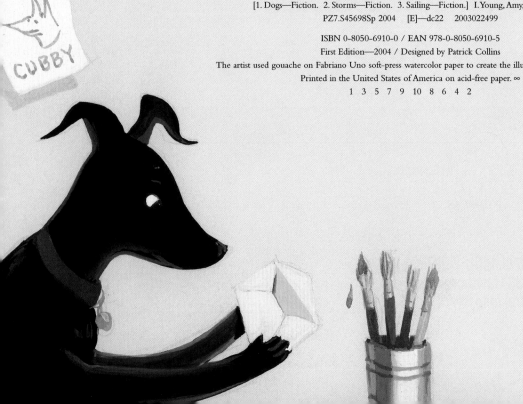

For Pook,
David, Jacob,
Kate, Annie, Mikhail
——H. S.

For pound puppies
and the people who love them,
and for Paul
——A. L. Y.

Cubby was hard at work on his new book, *Dogs of the Sea*. He had just finished the first half of the first sentence when the phone rang. It was Spike the artist, his best friend.

"How are you doing, Cubs? Do you want to take a break?" Spike asked.

"I really shouldn't right now," Cubby answered. "I'm at
work. You should be working, too!"

"But I just got an invitation to the grand opening of Ice
Cream Island," Spike said. "We have to go! It'll only take five
minutes to get there. I'll be right over."

When Spike got to Cubby's house he called out, "Are you ready to go?"

Inside, Cubby was sharpening his pencils. He didn't want to stop working. But he wasn't getting much done. It was such a beautiful day outside.

"Come on, Cubby," Spike pleaded. "Take a break."

Cubby tried to keep up as Spike raced down the street toward the ferry that would take them to Ice Cream Island.

When they arrived at the dock, they were *very* surprised. In big bold letters a sign read NO DOGS ON FERRY.

"No dogs? What are we going to do?" Spike cried.

Cubby thought they should just go home.

"Hey, hey, hey!" barked Spike to the ferry captain. "We need to cross!"

The ferry captain and his porters paid no attention to Spike.

Cubby and Spike were upset. It didn't seem fair.

The great giant ice cream cone was visible across Torch Lake. In the distance Ice Cream Island sparkled, so new and sugary, so shiny and pink.

"Hey, Cubby, that's the all-you-can-eat supercone," Spike drooled. "It's real!"

Cubby felt hunger pangs. "It looks delicious," he sighed.

Just then, Spike spotted something nearby. Sailboats in shades of red and blue and silver lined an old wooden pier. Spike had an idea. "Follow me!" he said to Cubby.

In a matter of minutes they had rented a boat from Myra. "Be very careful," she cautioned. "Experienced sailors only." "We're experienced sailors," Spike said as he waved.

"Spike, do you know how to sail?" Cubby asked.

"Of course I know how to sail," Spike answered. "Hang on!"

"I didn't know that. When did you learn how to sail?" Cubby asked politely.

Suddenly, a surprising gust of wind sent the boat flying across Torch Lake.

"We're sailing!" Spike yelled.

Cubby was a little worried. The boat was rocking wildly to and fro.

Spike wasn't paying attention to the tiller, the sails, or the lines. "We'll be there soon!" he shouted, proud on the prow.

"We're going to capsize! Spike, please help me steer this boat!" Cubby cried. He dove for the controls and leaned against the tiller with all his might.

The wind howled. It started to rain. Hard! Cubby struggled to steer the little boat. And then a flash of lightning lit the sky.

Spike didn't mind lightning. But he hated thunder.

KABA KABOOM BOOM BOOM!

Thunder wrapped around the little boat,
banging like a drum.
"Make it stop, make it stop," Spike whimpered.
Cubby remained as calm as he could.

The sails snapped and flapped in the
squall. The waves crashed and lurched.
And then a blast of north wind piled
the water into one enormous wave...

. . . that flung the small boat and flipped it upside down.

Cubby was tossed into the wind.

Spike was thrown into the roiling seas of Torch Lake.

It was a terrible, terrible moment.

"Spike! Spike!" Cubby called as loud as he could.
But there was no sign of his friend.

"Here I am, here I am," Spike yelped. He admitted he was a swimmer, not a sailor.

"Good," Cubby said. "Because you'll need to tow us. And it won't be easy."

As the fog lifted, Cubby looked ahead. "Spike, do you see what I see?"

"ICE CREAM ISLAND!" they both shouted together.

Right in front of them Ice Cream Island stood tall. It hadn't been touched by the storm. Spike and Cubby were so excited— and hungry!

Within minutes of arriving Cubby ordered the Perfection Parfait.

Spike ordered a Spumoni Baloney Grande.

"Would that be with the burger bits on top? Or swirled in?" the server asked with a smile.

"Swirled in," Spike quickly decided.

Over ice cream the dogs talked about their wild adventure.

"Ooh, stormy weather!" Spike said, rocking his sundae bowl. "Tell again how I was towing the boat. All by myself. With you standing on it! Tell that part."

Cubby told the whole story—how Spike was sucked into the water and how Cubby flew like a little balloon into the dark heart of it all. He told about the giant waves and how he was flung right through the thunder. And how happy he was to see Spike safe.

"Will you tell it to me one more time?" Spike asked.

"I sure will, Spike."

It was a wonderful, wonderful moment.

The next day Cubby woke up at the crack of dawn and went straight to work.

He wrote the second half of his first sentence with ease, then the rest of the book. *Dogs of the Sea* seemed to write itself.

"I'm ready to see your illustrations," Cubby said when Spike called that afternoon.

"You sound like you need to take a break!" Spike said.

"Oh, no—I'm working," Cubby explained.

"Just think—Ice Cream Island! It will only take five minutes!"

"Let's do it," said Cubby.

And off they went.